# Disney · PIXAR
# SOUL

## Read-Along
### STORYBOOK AND CD

Joe Gardner's jazz dreams are about to come true. But before he can step onstage, he takes a fateful step into the unknown. You can read along with me in your book. You will know it's time to turn the page when you hear this sound. . . . Let's begin now.

Published by Disney Press, an imprint of Disney Book Group. No part of this book may be reproduced or transmitted in any form or by any means, electronic or mechanical, including photocopying, recording, or by any information storage and retrieval system, without written permission from the publisher. For information address Disney Press, 1200 Grand Central Avenue, Glendale, California 91201.
Printed in the United States of America
First Paperback Edition, May 2020
1 3 5 7 9 10 8 6 4 2
Library of Congress Control Number: 2019952674
FAC-038091-20101
ISBN 978-1-368-05792-9
For more Disney Press fun, visit www.disneybooks.com

## DISNEY PRESS
Los Angeles • New York

**Joe Gardner** fought the urge to cover his ears. His middle school band students were playing a basic jazz number, but they couldn't keep up, keep time, or keep still.

That same day, Joe learned that his part-time teaching job had been made full-time. But Joe's dream was to *play* jazz. He believed it was what he was born to do—his true purpose.

Later that day, Joe's phone rang. It was Curley Baker, one of Joe's former students. He told Joe that he was the new drummer for the Dorothea Williams Quartet.

"Wow, I would die a happy man if I could perform with Dorothea Williams."

What Curley said next made Joe's heart beat faster. "Well, this could be your lucky day!"

Joe hurried to the legendary jazz club, The Half Note, to audition with the quartet.

When it was time for his solo, Joe closed his eyes, took a deep breath, and let the music flow. Afterward, Joe saw that everyone had stopped to listen.

"Uh, sorry, I zoned out a little back there. Heh."

Dorothea Williams smiled. "Get a suit, Teach. A good suit. Back here tonight. First show's at nine. Sound check's at seven. We'll see how you do."

Joe walked through the city, chatting on his cell phone and sharing the good news. "You're never gonna believe what just happened! I did it. I got the gig!" Just then, Joe saw a motorcycle heading right for him. He quickly stepped out of the way—and fell into an open manhole.

Joe's fall landed him on a moving
sidewalk headed for a bright light in the
distance. It was The Great Beyond! He
turned and ran away from the light. "I'm
not finished! I gotta get back! I don't
wanna die!"

Joe ripped through a barrier and
started falling again.

This time Joe landed in a beautiful, bright meadow. A counselor named Jerry appeared and welcomed Joe to the You Seminar, where new souls prepared for life on Earth.

Jerry thought Joe was a lost mentor— a soul who had lived an amazing and inspiring life. Mentors helped new souls find their Spark and earn their Earth Pass.

Getting an Earth Pass would be Joe's ticket home!

Meanwhile, high above
the moving sidewalk, the You
Seminar's accountant named
Terry counted the souls as
they passed by. Suddenly,
she stopped. "There's a soul
missing. The count's off."

Thinking Joe was a lost mentor, the counselors assigned him a troublesome soul known as 22.

"How many times do I have to tell you? I don't wanna go to Earth!"

22 had already been through hundreds of mentors, but Joe was unlike the others. He wanted to go *back* to Earth. 22 couldn't believe it! She agreed to give him her Earth Pass as soon as they found her Spark.

The pair made their way to The Hall of Everything. "Baking could be your Spark." But nothing about baking inspired 22. She tried other professions, but still no Spark and no Earth Pass.

"You told me you'd try."

"What can I say, Joe? Earth is boring."

22 had another idea. She took Joe to the Astral Plane, and introduced Joe to a crew of quirky characters, the Mystics, led by Moonwind. Though the Mystics' minds were in the Astral Plane, their bodies were still on Earth.

The Mystics, in the habit of helping lost souls, helped Joe open a portal to Earth. Joe closed his eyes, focusing on his body on Earth.

When he opened them again, Joe could see himself lying in a hospital bed, a therapy cat curled in his lap. Joe was ready to jump through, but Moonwind was worried.

"N-n-no, Joe! Don't rush this! It's not the right time!"

Joe jumped anyway, accidentally knocking 22 into the portal with him.

"AHHH!"

A moment later, Joe cautiously opened his eyes. The good news was that he was in a body. The bad news? He was in the wrong body!

"No! No! No! No! No! NO! I'm in the cat? Wait a minute—if I'm in here, then who . . ." Joe looked at his body. 22 was in there, and she was horrified!

"I'm in a body! Nooo!"

Joe did his best to stay calm. This was all Moonwind's fault, he decided.

"Okay. Gotta find Moonwind. He can fix this."

After escaping the hospital, Joe and 22 ended up on the streets of New York. 22 was rattled by the hustle and bustle of the city streets. She sat Joe's body down and swore she'd never move again.

Joe darted off, snagging a slice of pizza. 22 wolfed it down and, to her surprise, felt much better.

The two soon found Moonwind at an intersection spinning his sign. The Mystic promised he would get Joe back into his body. "See you at The Half Note at 6:30. I'll take care of everything!"

Once they got to Joe's apartment, there was a knock on the door. It was Connie, from Joe's music class. She told Joe that she wanted to quit the trombone. But when Connie played, it was clear she loved music. She just needed a little encouragement to stick with it.

22 was feeling something she'd never felt before—*inspired*.

"I'll help you, but I . . . wanna try a few things while we're here. If Connie can find something she loves, maybe I can, too."

22 dressed in Joe's trusty old brown suit and, after a mishap with some electric hair clippers, hurried to visit Dez at Buddy's Barbershop.

22 liked sitting in the barber's chair. She soon had the whole room gossiping, laughing, and even philosophizing with her. No one had ever seen that side of Joe before!

22 was finally feeling comfortable in Joe's body when an unexpected gust of wind knocked Joe's hat off. As 22 bent over to grab it, Joe's pants ripped at the seam! There was only one place where they could get the pants fixed in a hurry: Joe's mom's tailor shop.

Joe's mom, Libba, had heard about his upcoming performance with the Dorothea Williams Quartet. She was upset he was chasing an impossible goal. But for the first time, Joe was ready to tell his mom exactly what his dream meant to him. He leaned in and told 22 just what to say.

"Look, if I'm doin' what I love, no matter how hard that is, I'll be fine."

Libba listened and smiled. Then, instead of sewing up Joe's pants, she opened the closet and pulled out a surprise.

"That's my dad's suit."

As Joe and 22 waited for Moonwind outside The Half Note, 22 watched a maple seed slowly spin to the ground. She admitted she was beginning to like being on Earth. Maybe she hadn't found her Spark in The Hall of Everything because her Spark was walking, or sky watching.

Joe disagreed. Those couldn't be her Spark. They weren't a real purpose. She would just have to try again when she got back to the You Seminar.

"No. No. I-I've gotta find it here. On Earth. This is my only chance to find my Spark!"

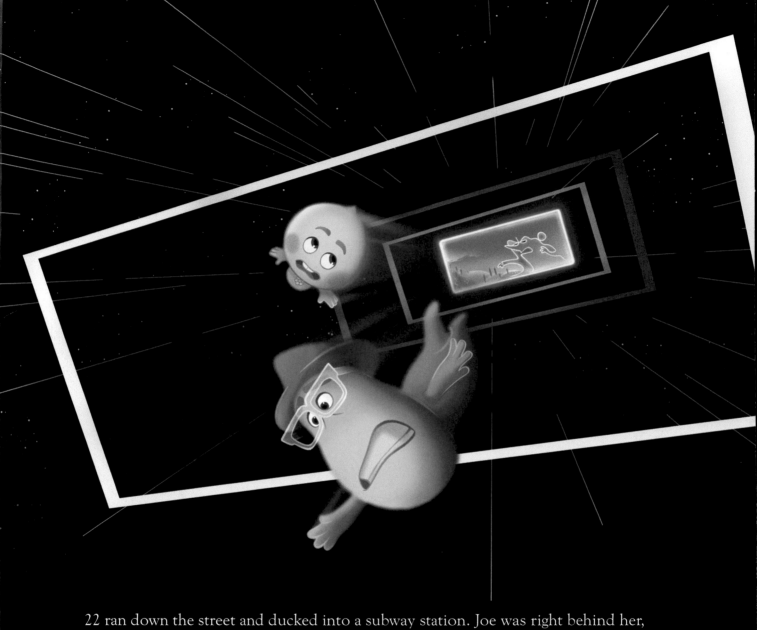

22 ran down the street and ducked into a subway station. Joe was right behind her, meowing furiously. Then, out of nowhere, Terry appeared.

"There you are, Joe Gardner. It's your time to go."

A portal scooped up Joe and 22, and their souls returned to the You Seminar.

Joe was upset. He'd been moments away from finally playing with Dorothea Williams.

Suddenly, the counselors were congratulating 22. She had earned her Earth Pass! But the young soul still had no idea what her Spark was.

22 handed Joe the Earth Pass.

"It filled in because I was in your body, being *you*. It's your Spark that changed it, not mine."

22 slipped away, leaving Joe alone at the portal's edge. Curious, Joe asked one of the counselors what 22's purpose was, what had finally completed her Earth Pass. The counselor just laughed. They didn't assign purposes to souls!

Joe refused to believe the counselor. After all, music *was* his purpose. It's what he was meant to do! Joe took the Earth Pass and jumped into the portal.

Back on Earth, Joe sat at The Half Note piano as the Dorothea Williams Quartet took the stage. From his first note to the last, Joe played his heart out. He was in perfect sync with the other musicians, and his solos brought the house down! It was everything Joe had dreamed.

But later, after the show, Joe felt strangely unfulfilled. He thought playing with the quartet would make him feel different somehow, but it didn't. Nothing had changed.

Back at his apartment, Joe sat at his piano. He noticed his pocket was filled with items 22 had gathered during her day on Earth. He dumped the objects next to the piano and began to play. As he pressed the keys, he considered the items. They looked so small and ordinary, but they were reminders of the little things that 22 loved about life.

As Joe played more intently, he closed his eyes, his focus grew, and he entered the Zone. Then, when he opened his eyes, he was back on the Astral Plane.

Moonwind was waiting for Joe. Something was wrong . . . 22 wasn't herself. She had become a lost soul, angry and destructive. The enraged soul rampaged through the You Seminar. No one could stop her!

"No! Wait, 22! I was wrong!" Joe apologized, promising 22 she *was* ready for Earth. But 22 couldn't hear him. In a last, desperate attempt, Joe reached out and placed a maple seed in 22's hand—a reminder of her love for Earth.

Finally, 22 began to calm. Joe gave 22 back her Earth Pass and walked her to the edge of the Earth Portal.

"But we never found out what filled in my last box."

Joe smiled. "It doesn't matter. It's what you do with it that counts."

He promised to stay with 22 as long as he could. "Relax. I've done this before. Ready?"

22 and Joe leapt into the portal, and 22's Earth Pass began to glow. He smiled reassuringly as she let go of his hand and Joe returned, once more, to The Great Beyond.

Joe was back on the moving sidewalk when Counselor Jerry stopped him. Joe had inspired all the counselors, and they had a special gift for him. An Earth Portal materialized beside the sidewalk.

And so, Joe took one more fateful step, unsure of what lay ahead, but prepared to appreciate each and every moment of his wonderful life.